MINGO

by Lenice U. Strohmeier • illustrated by Bill Farnsworth

MARSHALL CAVENDISH   NEW YORK

I would like to thank Pat Lowery Collins, Ellen Wittlinger,
Chris Jones, Laurie Jacobs, Chris Doyle, Donna McArdle,
and my editors, Margery Cuyler and Judith Whipple, for
all their encouragement and advice on the manuscript.
I also wish to thank Julius Lester for granting permission
to reprint part of his introduction to *To Be a Slave*
(New York: Dial Books, 1998).
—L.U.S

Marshall Cavendish, 99 White Plains Road, Tarrytown, NY 10591
www.marshallcavendish.com

The text of this book is set in 14 point Berkeley Oldstyle Medium.
The illustrations are rendered using oils on canvas.
Pinted in China
First edition
1 2 3 4 5 6

Library of Congress Cataloging-in-Publication Data
Strohmeier, Lenice U.
Mingo / by Lenice U. Strohmeier ; illustrations by Bill Farnsworth.
p. cm.
Summary: In Massachusetts in 1771, seven-year-old Olivia learns
about freedom from her father's slave, Mingo, who was promised
that he'd be freed when the tide was low enough that he could
walk to a certain spot offshore.
ISBN 0-7614-5111-0
[1. Slavery—Fiction. 2. Freedom—Fiction. 3. Massachusetts—
History—Colonial period, ca. 1600-1775—Fiction.]
I. Farnsworth, Bill, ill. II. Title.
PZ7.S92153 Mi 2002 [Fic]—dc21 2002007847

For John, L.J., and Brie and anyone who's kept a vigil by the sea
—L.U.S.

For Deb and Lauren
—B.F.

Of course, my underlying and hidden purpose was simply this:
If a child could experience slaves as human beings, then it might
be possible for that same child to look at the descendants of slaves
and also see another human being, no more, no less.

—Julius Lester from his new introduction to the
thirtieth anniversary edition of *To Be a Slave*

I think I was five when I first noticed that Mingo always went to the window or down to the beach at low tide—dead low tide. He'd stand and stare at Aunt Becky's Ledge for a few minutes as if in prayer. Then he'd return to work.

Robin Mingo was my father's slave and my friend. He taught me to recognize birds by their songs. His favorite was the mockingbird.

"They're always happy, Miss Olivia," he'd say, his brown eyes sparkling like the sea, "singing just for the joy of it and not caring that none of the songs are their own."

When I turned seven, it was a warm autumn day in the year 1771. Father was on his ship traveling to China. I waved to him when *Marinette* sailed past our house, wondering how long he'd be gone and if this place called China was anything like Massachusetts. Mother dabbed at her tears all morning and tried to keep busy pickling cabbage, beets, and cucumbers with Deborah, Mingo's wife. The kitchen was dark and filled with the odor of vinegar. Outside the air was full of light and the smells of the ocean, but there wasn't anything to do. At noon, Mingo went down to the beach. I followed.

"What are you looking at?" I asked, taking off my mobcap and letting my hair swirl in the warm offshore breeze.

"It's not what I'm looking at, it's what I'm looking for," he said.

"Did you lose something?"

"Freedom," he said, rubbing the gray hair that curled above his ears. "I'm looking for freedom."

"Are you going to sail away?"

"No." He stretched out his arms. "But if I had wings, I'd fly."

"You mean, like a bird?"

"Like a bird or an angel. It doesn't really matter. Freedom is freedom, and I'll take it any way it comes."

"I don't understand."

Mingo placed his hand on my shoulder. "Your grandfather promised me that if ever the tide was low enough so a man. . ." He hesitated and added, "or girl could walk out to Aunt Becky's Ledge, he'd give me my freedom."

"Could that happen? Could the tide ever be that low?"

"It happened the day I came here from Portsmouth. I was just a boy, a little older than you, Miss Olivia," he said. "Your grandfather believed the strange tide was an omen, a sign from heaven about my arrival, so he gave me his promise, and we left it in God's hands."

"Grandfather's dead."

"Yes, but everything he owned was passed on to your father —his slaves, land, and promises."

From that time on, at dead low tide, I joined Mingo to look out at the sea. He looked for freedom, and I always hoped that it wouldn't be there. I wanted him to stay here with me forever.

We checked once a day, except if the moon was a sliver of a crescent or as round as a coin. Then we'd check twice. One night, shivering against the star-studded sky, I asked Mingo why.

He took off his jacket, wrapped the worn cloth around my shoulders, and said, "The tides are always lower when there is a new or full moon."

"Then why do we have to check every day?"

"The sea isn't Mabel the dairy cow. She's unpredictable with a mind of her own, and I have to watch her closely."

"Me too," I said, then yawned and rubbed my eyes. "Besides, it's more fun than cross-stitching samplers or practicing lettering."

The only time we didn't bother checking was during fall northeasters. Even at low tide, the angry sea churned breakers that rolled and crashed over Aunt Becky's Ledge. Once in a

while, because we liked the sting of rain and wind on our faces,
we'd walk out to the bluff and watch the waves pound against
the beach until Mother called me in for prayers or lessons.

On winter days, when snowdrifts tickled the windowsills, we'd climb to the widow's walk and rub peepholes on frosted panes. As the tide turned, Mingo would sing. It was always the same song: "Swing low, sweet chariot, comin' for to carry me home; Swing low, sweet chariot, comin' for to carry me home." He called it a spiritual.

"Is that your very own song?"

"Only when I'm singing it."

"I want to learn it, so it will be my song, too."

By the time winter snows melted into spring wildflowers, I had learned the spiritual. One morning I was singing it, skipping barefoot through dandelions and dew, when I heard chirping by the root cellar. I bent down and pushed aside the wet grass. Staring up at me was a baby bird. His beak opened as if he would swallow up the sky. I picked up the warm, featherless body and felt his heart beating against my fingers. Tucking him into my mobcap, I held him next to my chest and ran to find Mingo.

"A baby mockingbird," Mingo said, leaning a pitchfork against the door to Mabel's stall. "He's lucky you've found him, Miss Olivia. He needs you to feed him and keep him safe until the day he can fly away."

"I'll feed him and keep him safe, but I won't let him fly away."

"Someday you will," Mingo said. "But first you'll have to fill his belly and give him a safe place to sleep."

Mingo showed me how to dig for worms and drop them into the baby bird's mouth. Then he helped me make a cage out of twigs, with a nest made of hay and horsehair.

"Now all he needs is a name," said Mingo. "And you best put your cap back on before Mistress Elsbeth sees you."

"His name is Sam," I said, covering the cage with my baby quilt. "And Mother doesn't care if I wear this silly thing or not."

Sam was always hungry. I fed him berries, bugs, and, once in a while, warm cornmeal from the kitchen when Deborah wasn't looking.

By summer, Sam wasn't little anymore, and his feathers had turned gray and white. I let him fly around my room at night and took him to the beach every day, where we'd wait together for Mingo and the low tide.

One afternoon as the fog billowed in from the sea, Mingo said, "Sam's ready for freedom, Miss Olivia."

"Well, I'm not," I said, picking up the cage.

Mingo bent down, rubbing his sore knee. "Someday you will be, Miss Olivia. And someday you'll know that keeping another soul caged is wrong. Our hearts are free even if our bodies are not. It's in your hands."

I walked back to the house, Mingo's words bouncing around in my head. As I stepped into the kitchen, Mother snapped at me for losing my cap and missing noon tea with Mistress Sarah and her boring son Thomas.

One hot autumn day with the odor of clam flats papering the moist air, I sat on the beach singing to Sam. "Swing low, sweet

chariot. . ." When I finished, the lapping waves sounded far, far away. I turned and looked out at the ledge. Rocks that I had never seen before, rocks that were always covered by water, lay glistening in the sun. A little farther and Mingo could walk out to Aunt Becky's Ledge. But where was he? I ran up the bluff and across the field to the house.

"Deborah," I said, trying to stop my ragged breathing, "where's Mingo?"

"He's unloading *Marinette*, could be home anytime. What's the matter, child?"

"Olivia, it's time for practicing letters with the quill," Mother twittered from the pantry.

I didn't answer. Instead I ran out the kitchen door, back to the beach, and sat next to Sam. I tried to decide what to do, while I stared at the sand sifting through my fingers. Thoughts drifted back and forth in my head like seaweed in a gentle current. Then, all of a sudden, I knew.

I blinked hard, trying to stop the tears, and bent over to take off my shoes.

At first, the boulders were dry and gritty against the bottom of my feet. Farther out, they became slippery and covered with greenish-black slime. I fell twice and cut my legs on barnacles, but I continued crawling toward Aunt Becky's Ledge. Almost there, I stopped at a large gap in the rocks. The water didn't look very deep, but I was afraid.

I sat down and dangled my feet above the lapping waves, wishing I were brave enough to wade through the water to the dry rocks and seagulls on the other side. I sat and sat until water began splashing around my ankles. The tide was coming in. This wasn't the one Mingo was looking for. I stood up and turned toward the beach. My heart pounded as I started back over the rocks.

Not far from shore, I saw more and more rocks disappearing beneath the waves. I'd have to hurry and wade the rest of the way. My cuts stung as I put my legs into the saltwater, where tentacles of seaweed coiled around them. Inching lower, my toes scraped against a granite boulder. I pushed away from the rock and tried to stand up. But I pushed too hard, falling into the ocean.

Saltwater swirled up my nose into my mouth and burned my throat as I tried to cough. I felt around for a rock, something to stand on, but my legs were heavy and wouldn't behave. I clawed toward the sky, but my fingers never left the sea. Then something grabbed me around the waist, pulled me through the water toward the surface, and lifted me into the air. I coughed and sneezed.

"Miss Olivia, you scared me half to death. What made you come out here?"

"I thought it was the tide, your tide." I sneezed again and continued, "Grandfather said that if a man or girl could walk out to Aunt Becky's Ledge, you'd have your freedom."

Mingo hugged me, and I hugged him back. He carried me above the waves toward the beach and home. Mother and Deborah gave me warm soup and wrapped me in soft blankets. Father dismissed Mingo and then paced before me with an icy speech about the sea and how I should stay away. He said that Grandfather's promise to Mingo was in God's hands and not mine.

Why not? I thought. But instead I asked, "Why isn't Mingo's freedom in your hands?"

"Because I must honor my father's wishes as you must honor mine." He turned to leave. The loud smack of his boots against the pine floor followed him as he walked away.

The seasons tumbled by. Mingo's hair turned the color of winter fog, and he used a cane to steady his stride. But we still kept the vigil—Mingo, Sam, and I.

Then, one day in spring, when the birds started to sing late into the night and again very early in the morning, Mingo got sick. I begged Deborah for two days before she finally brought me to their cabin. Mingo lay very still in the old oak bed. I tucked the quilt under his chin, and his eyes opened.

"Ah, Miss Olivia and Master Sam," he said, before licking his dry lips. "It's good to see you."

"We miss you," I whispered, lifting Sam's cage onto the faded quilt. When Mingo reached up, pushing his fingers through the bars, Sam hopped down from his perch and started to sing.

"Such a sad song for such a pretty bird," Mingo sighed. He turned and looked out the window. "Will you do something for me?" he asked. "The new moon is tomorrow. Would you check the tides?"

"Yes. But you'll be better soon, and we can check the tides together again."

He turned back to me and smiled, but his eyes no longer sparkled like the sea.

Early the next morning, before the sun peeked over the horizon, Deborah stopped me in the kitchen. Her cheeks were damp and her voice was soft.

"Miss Olivia, ain't no more checking of tides to be done. Mingo's about to close his eyes in this world for the last time."

I went outside, carrying Sam's cage, and stood in the morning twilight. My body felt heavy, as if my clothes were soaked with seawater, and tears flooded my eyes. I stared out at Aunt Becky's Ledge.

Everything was blurry and out of focus. With my mobcap, I wiped the tears away and looked out at the rocks again.

It was low tide, the lowest I'd ever seen. It was the one Mingo was looking for.

While I stood alone, wishing away this day, this dead low tide, Sam started to sing. I took off my shoes, picked up the cage, and stepped up on a boulder. My body felt lighter.

Walking and slipping over seaweed and barnacles, I finally made it out to Aunt Becky's Ledge. This was a place I'd never been before. I couldn't hear Mabel mooing or the wagons rattling down Hale Street to the clip-clop of horses' hooves—just the music of waves, Sam's sad song, and the beating of my heart.

Opening the cage door, I slipped my hand inside, and Sam stopped singing. He hopped onto my finger. I lifted him out into the light, where no shadows of cage bars fell across his feathers. He cocked his head, looked around, and started to sing again. This time it was a happy song, but it made me sad. Sam stretched out his wings. Then, without a sound, he flew away.

I reached toward the sky, aching to pull Sam and Mingo back. But knowing that I couldn't, I hugged the emptiness in my arms and listened to the wind snapping the sleeves of my dress.

"I love you," I whispered.

Then I heard singing. It was soft at first and it gradually rose, pure and clear above the waves. "Swing low, sweet chariot, comin' for to carry me. . ." I held my breath, closed my eyes, and turned around. Opening my eyes, I blinked hard and saw only the fierce morning light as it bounced off the wet rocks and rolling sea.

At that moment, Deborah started ringing the old ship's bell beside the kitchen door. I felt certain it must mean one thing. Mingo was finally free. I imagined him with wings, as tears rolled down my cheeks, and I finished our song, "A band of angels comin' after me, comin' for to carry me home."

Author's Note

In Pride's Crossing, a section of Beverly, Massachusetts, there is a place called Mingo Beach. In 1974, an elderly neighbor told me the legend of Robin Mingo. Haunted by the tale, I could never pass the beach without looking for that special low tide, and I promised my family that someday I'd write Mingo's story. Not knowing where to begin, I found the voice of Olivia, a fictional character, who showed me the way. Now the story belongs to both characters.

Mingo's life is mostly a mystery, and I can't be sure the tale on which my story is based ever happened. The recorded history from two hundred-plus years ago is sparse and contains inconsistencies. According to the Beverly Vital Records, Robin Mingo, a slave of Thomas Woodbury, married Deborah Tailor, a West Indian, on June 20, 1707. On July 15, 1722, Mingo was baptized at the First Parish Church, Beverly. At my request, Charles Wainwright, Chairman of the Church Historical Committee, located the original handwritten baptismal certificate in their archives. However, I found two different dates for Mingo's death in the Beverly Vital Records. One, attributed to the First Parish Church, states that he was buried in 1773 and was the property of Captain Nicholas Thorndike. The other, a private record kept by Colonel Robert Hale, Parish Clerk for the First Parish Church, and James Hill, says that Mingo died in 1748 and Deborah in 1759.

After murder, slavery is the worst sin man can commit. In 1754, Beverly was home to twenty-eight slaves. They were property and, upon their owners' discretion, could be sold, willed, or freed. The town did not create laws concerning slaves but relied on those formed by the Province of Massachusetts Bay in New England that required slaves to be off the streets after nine at night and prohibited them from marrying whites, voting, and joining the militia. However, slaves in Massachusetts had some rights that those in southern colonies were denied. They could sue anyone, and several sued owners for their freedom and won. They also had the right to make contracts, have a jury trial, testify in court against anyone, and purchase and own property. In 1783, Massachusetts finally abolished slavery.

To fully understand and experience the horrors of slavery, further reading on the subject is necessary. I want to thank Julius Lester for permission to recommend his books *From Slave Ship to Freedom Road* and *To Be a Slave*. I also recommend *They Came in Chains* by Milton Meltzer and *Many Thousand Gone: African Americans from Slavery to Freedom* by Virginia Hamilton.   – Lenice U. Strohmeier